WASPS

ASHLEY GISH

INSECTS X BOOKS

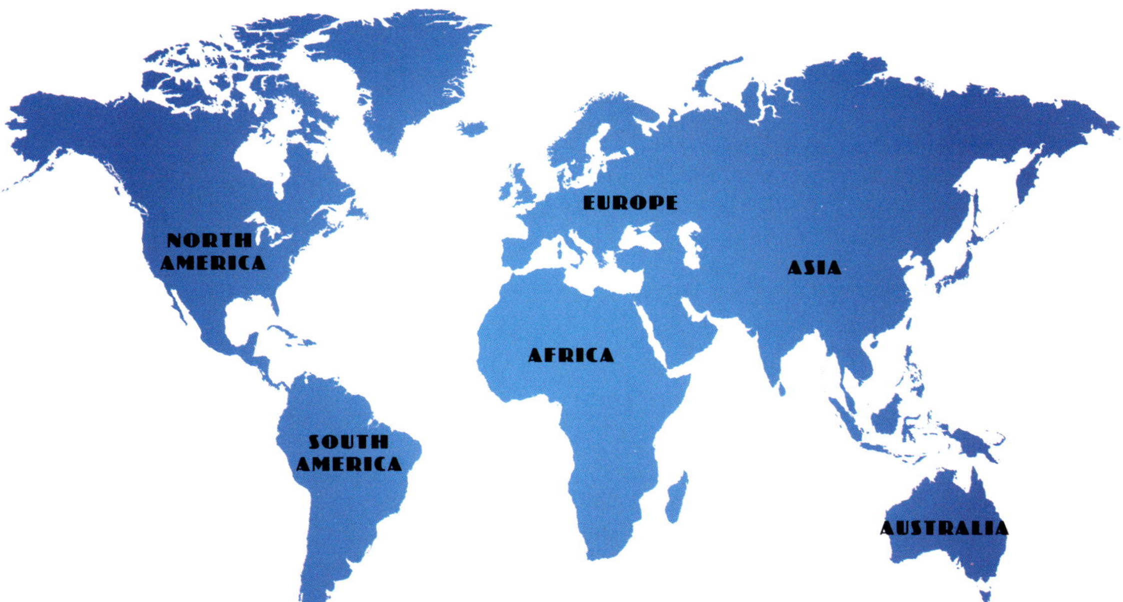

CREATIVE EDUCATION · CREATIVE PAPERBACKS

Published by Creative Education and Creative Paperbacks · P.O. Box 227, Mankato, Minnesota 56002 · Creative Education and Creative Paperbacks are imprints of The Creative Company · www.thecreativecompany.us · Design by Rita Marshall · Production by Chelsey Luther · Printed in the United States of America · Photographs by Alamy (Jason Bazzano, FLPA, imageBROKER, Zoonar GmbH), Dreamstime (Natalia Bachkova, Ekaterina Balashova, Viter8, Yodke67), FreeVectorMaps.com, Getty Images (Eric Lowenbach/Moment Open, SilvanBachmann/RooM, VW Pics/Universal Images Group), iStockphoto (Antagain, Henrik_L, mikespics, MilaSCH, Trifonov_Evgeniy), Minden Pictures (Piotr Naskrecki, Daniele Occhiato/Buiten-beeld), PLoS ONE (Bernhard Schurian), Shutterstock (Eric Isselee, Stephen Marques)

 • Library of Congress Cataloging-in-Publication Data • Names: Gish, Ashley, author. • Title: Wasps / Ashley Gish. • Series: X-Books: Insects. • Includes index. • Summary: A countdown of five of the most fascinating wasps provides thrills as readers learn about the biological, social, and hunting characteristics of these colorful, stinging insects. • Identifiers: LCCN 2017060043 / ISBN 978-1-60818-994-6 (hardcover) / ISBN 978-1-62832-621-5 (pbk) / ISBN 978-1-64000-095-7 (eBook) • Subjects: LCSH: Wasps—Juvenile literature. • Classification: LCC SB945.W3 G57 2018 / DDC 595.79—dc23

CCSS: RI.3.1-8; RI.4.1-5, 7; RI.5.1-3, 8; RI.6.1-2, 4, 7; RH.6-8.3-8

First Edition HC 9 8 7 6 5 4 3 2 1 • First Edition PBK 9 8 7 6 5 4 3 2 1

WASPS

CONTENTS

ABDOMEN
THORAX
WINGS
HEAD
STINGER
MANDIBLE

XCEPTIONAL INSECTS

Wasps are skilled insects. They can fly quickly. Their bodies are beautifully colored. Some are dangerous hunters. There are more than 30,000 kinds of these extreme insects.

Wasp Basics

Wasps are insects. Like all insects, wasp bodies have three parts. These are the head, thorax, and abdomen. They have compound eyes. These are made up of many parts. They can see in all directions. Wasps use mouthparts called mandibles to clutch and chew food.

Two pairs of wings grow from a wasp's thorax. At the end of most female wasps' abdomens is a stinger. Stingers are used in defense and in hunting. Wasps can sting multiple times, causing severe pain.

WASP SIZE

Wasps are usually less than one inch (2.5 cm) long.

STINGING

Not all wasps sting. The stinging wasps belong to the Vespidae family.

THE TINKERBELL WASP

is the smallest wasp at only 0.01 inch (0.25 mm) long.

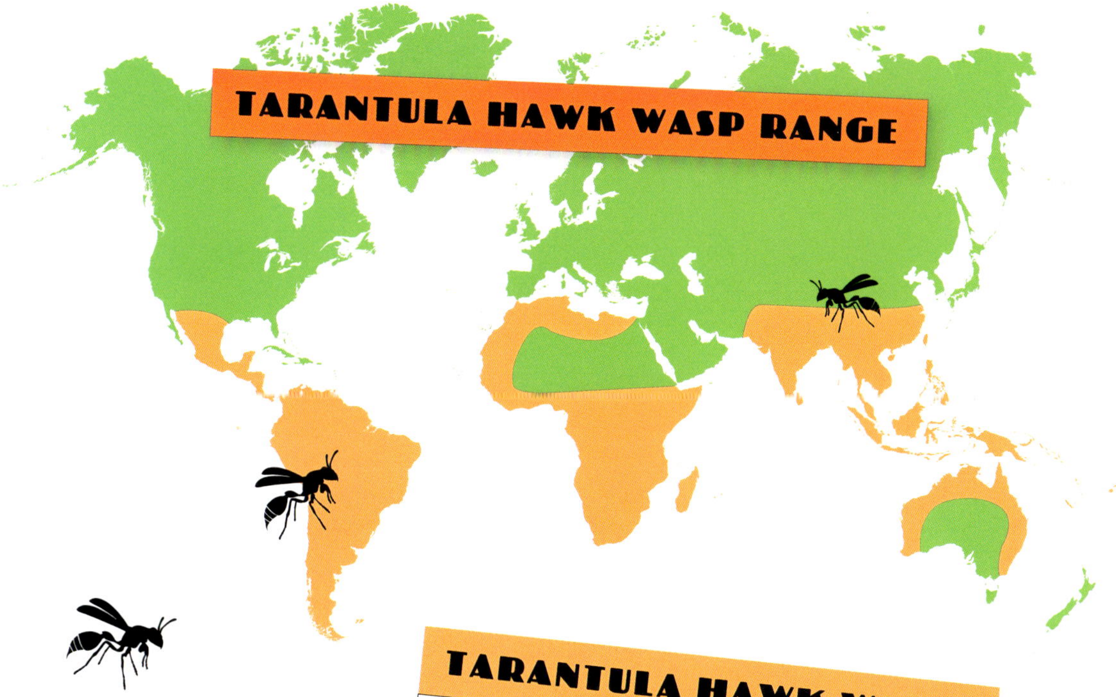

TARANTULA HAWK WASPS are the longest wasp **species**. They can be more than two inches (5.1 cm) long!

Wasp Colonies

Some wasps live in groups called colonies. A colony can have more than 5,000 members. They build a large nest. It is made of the wasps' saliva, water, and chewed-up wood.

Wasp bodies are protected by a hard exoskeleton. They can be multicolored, from yellow and black to red and white. Jewel wasps are metallic green. These colors warn the wasps' enemies to stay away.

Many wasps eat other insects. Some paralyze their meal with **venom**. When something is paralyzed, it is unable to move. Wasps hunt ants, cicadas, caterpillars, and other wasps. Some even eat spiders larger than themselves. Some wasps kill other insects only to feed baby wasps. Their own meal might include flower **nectar** or honeydew. Smaller insects such as aphids create honeydew when they poop.

GOOD RIDDANCE

Wasps eat or lay eggs inside pest insects.

WASP BASICS FACT

The largest wasp nest on record was 12 feet, 2 inches (3.7 m) long and 5 feet, 3 inches (1.6 m) wide.

TOP FIVE XTREME WASPS

Xtreme Wasp #5

Using Resources *Hymenoepimecis argyraphaga* lives in Costa Rica. It injects a substance into an orb-weaving spider. This puts the spider under the wasp's control. The spider carries the wasp's egg. The egg hatches, and the baby wasp sucks fluid from the spider. Then it forces the spider to spin a web. The baby wasp uses the spider's silk to wrap itself in a cocoon. When it emerges from the cocoon, it flies away to find nectar to eat.

In 2016, four new wasp species were found in China.

All lay their eggs in other wasps' and bees' nests.

Wasp Babies

Wasp babies are called larvae. They hatch from eggs laid by a female. They are soft and wingless. Some larvae are fed by worker wasps. Others eat whatever is around them. Sometimes, what's around them is the inside of another insect!

A female tarantula hawk wasp paralyzes a tarantula. Then she lays a single egg inside the spider. The larva eats the tarantula from the inside out. Once the larva has finished growing, it bursts out of the tarantula!

As larvae grow, they shed their skin. This is called molting. Larvae eat for about 22 days. Eventually, they spit out a substance called silk. They use this to spin a cocoon around themselves. Inside the cocoon, larvae are called pupae.

Pupae develop into adult wasps after about nine days. Pupae do not eat. All they do is grow. They develop legs, **antennae**, and wings. Females grow stingers. Soon, social wasps will join other wasps in a colony. Others will leave the nest and live alone.

spin g

Wasp queen starts laying eggs

20 days

Larvae hatch and molt

9 days

Pupae grow

winter
Adult workers come out of cocoons
New queens live as other wasps die

WASP BABIES FACT

The transformation from larva to pupa to adult is called metamorphosis.

TOP FIVE XTREME WASPS

Xtreme Wasp #4

Protective Odor The bone-house wasp builds its nest in tiny spaces under wood or junk piles. It lays its eggs in the nest's inner cells. Scientists recently discovered that this wasp kills ants and stuffs the outer cells of the nest with their dead bodies. This wall protects the eggs and larvae inside. Ants release a bad smell, even when dead. This keeps **predators** away.

XTRAORDINARY LIFESTYLE

Some wasps are social. They live in colonies. Others are solitary. They live alone. All wasps use extreme skills to build nests and find food.

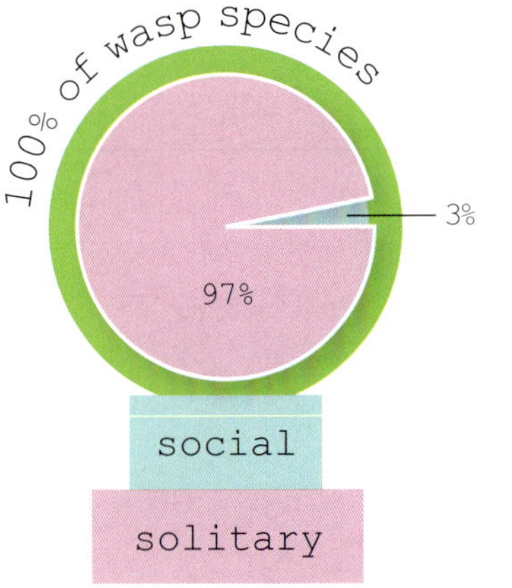

WASP SOCIETY FACT

When one queen dies, another female will take her place in the colony.

FAST FLIERS

Yellow jackets can fly up to 7 miles (11.3 km) per hour.

Wasp Society

Every year, social wasp colonies start from scratch. In the spring, the queen starts to build a nest. Then she lays eggs. These hatch into workers and drones. Workers are all females. They feed and protect the larvae. Drones mate with the queen.

When social wasps feel threatened, they can call on the colony for help. Their bodies produce scents that warn other wasps of danger.

Solitary wasps come together only to mate. Some females lay their eggs in a shared nest. These types of wasps build nests underground. They lay only a few eggs. Solitary wasp mothers bring food into the nest so that the larvae have something to eat after they hatch. Some of these wasps protect their larvae. Others do not.

XEMPLARY SKILLS

Wasps use many skills to thrive in the world. A good memory helps them locate food and get back home. Some wasps are talented fighters. Others are skilled tricksters. They may steal from other wasps or get them to raise their young.

XEMPLARY SKILLS FACT

The caramba wasp from Peru has a false ant head on the tip of its tail. This lures other insects to come close enough to be attacked.

Stump stabber wasps use their stingers to feel around inside the cracks of tree stumps. Once they feel a grub, they stab it and lay their eggs inside it.

Solitary wasps are fierce hunters. They attack spiders and insects much bigger than themselves. Many females lay eggs inside their catch. Some of the largest solitary wasps are cicada killer and spider hawk wasps. Each can grow to more than 1.5 inches (3.8 cm) long.

One kind of spider wasp, *Auplopus architectus*, chews off the legs of spiders. This makes carrying the spider easier. The blue-black spider wasp is a skilled thief. It steals food from the colonies of other wasps.

Solitary wasps take time to memorize where they live. They fly around their nest in a big circle to look for familiar rocks and twigs. After they have done this several times, they know where to find their nest. Now they will not get lost when they are out hunting for food!

TOP FIVE XTREME WASPS

Xtreme Wasp #3

Pest Control *Baryscapus dioryctriae* lives in the forests of northern China. This wasp lays eggs inside other insects. Scientists think the wasps may be used as weapons against beetles that destroy pine trees. The beetles' babies live inside the trees (shown), so poison that kills insects does not work against them. But the wasps lay their eggs inside the beetles' larvae. The wasp larvae kill the beetles before they have a chance to develop into adults!

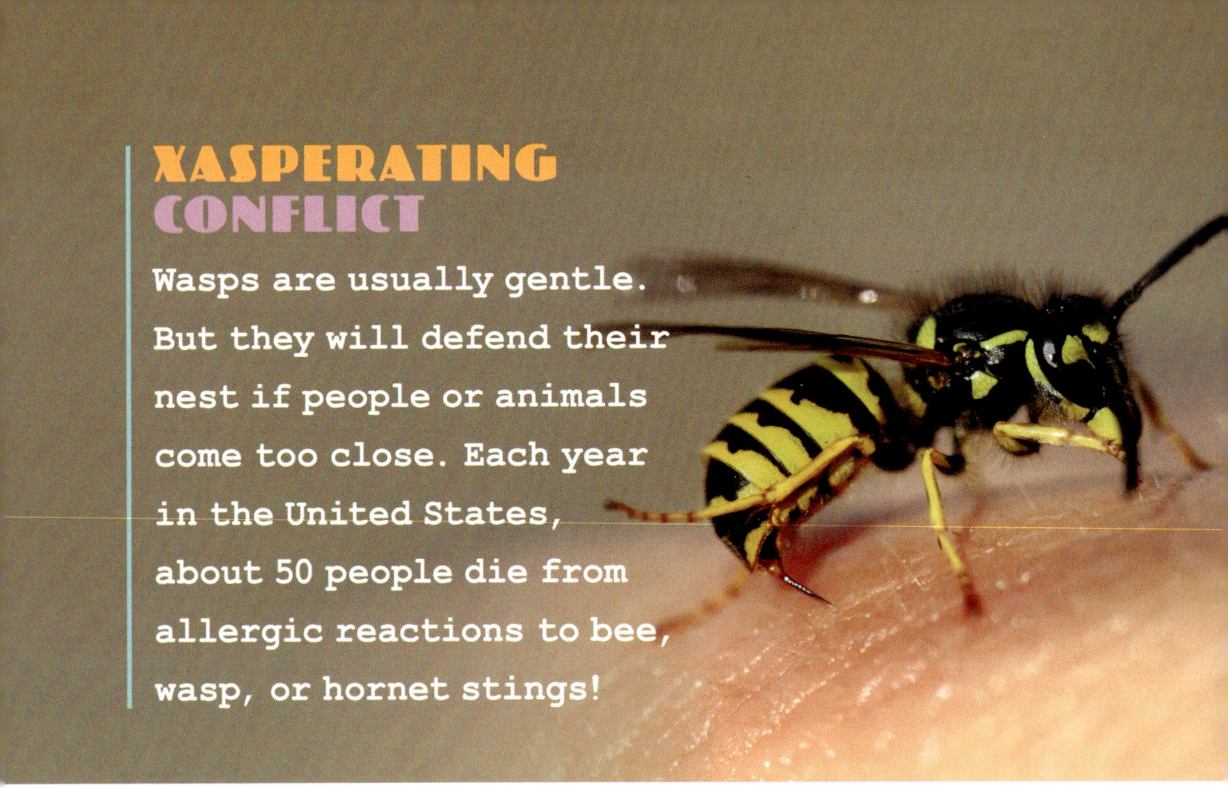

XASPERATING CONFLICT

Wasps are usually gentle. But they will defend their nest if people or animals come too close. Each year in the United States, about 50 people die from allergic reactions to bee, wasp, or hornet stings!

Wasp Survival

Many animals eat wasps and their larvae. Some birds eat adult wasps. They scrape the wasps against branches to remove their stingers. Raccoons and even bears attack wasp nests to eat the soft-bodied larvae inside.

In spring, wasps eat sweet honeydew produced by larvae. But by autumn, all the larvae have developed into adults. Wasps become aggressive at that time because they are looking for food outside the nest. People who are picnicking may be attacked by wasps. Yellow jackets are attracted to sugary drinks and fresh fruit. Their long tongues suck up sweet liquids.

Some people are known as "wasp-watchers." They enjoy watching solitary wasps hunt for food and build their underground nests.

Social wasps use their stingers for defense.

They are more aggressive than solitary wasps.

The relationship between parasite and host is important. A parasite is a plant or animal that lives inside or on another living thing, called a host. Parasites give nothing to the host. They often cause disease or death. The host provides a place for the parasite to live. Many wasp species are parasitoid. The larvae live inside other insects or plants. Most eventually kill their host.

WASP SURVIVAL FACT

Wasps do not store food.

Queens must rely on body fat to live through the winter.

TOP FIVE XTREME WASPS

Xtreme Wasp #2

Imposters! Velvet ants are actually a kind of wasp. Females are wingless. They are covered in colorful hair. The colors warn predators to stay away. These wasps also vibrate their bodies to create a squeaking sound. Velvet ants can release a bad smell, too. This usually scares away other insects. If all those defenses fail, a female velvet ant will use her stinger, which is half the length of her body!

XCITING FACTS

Members of a social colony fall into three categories: queen, worker, and drone.

The larvae of some wasp species produce a sweet fluid that is eaten by the adult wasps.

Pollen wasps build their nests underground. They feed their young nectar and pollen.

Cicada killer wasp tunnels can be up to 5.8 feet (1.8 m) long and 15 inches (38.1 cm) deep.

Wasps are easily mistaken for hornets, but they are different insects.

Pitcher plants trap and eat insects. Wasps are drawn to their sweet nectar.

Badgers are known to dig up ground-dwelling wasps' nests to devour larvae.

The Richteria fairyfly hunts underwater. Its racquet-shaped wings are used like paddles.

Solitary wasps are not usually aggressive toward people.

An insect that lived in Asia 100 million years ago had a cockroach body, grasshopper legs, ant antennae, and a wasp face.

Bee-eater birds (right) grab wasps and rub them against twigs to remove their stingers.

Mantidflies look like a cross between a wasp and a praying mantis. But they are not related to either.

For more than 100 years, until 2015, scientists thought the *Oobius depressus* wasp had died out.

Ants, bees, hornets, and

wasps are all closely related.

TOP FIVE XTREME WASPS

Xtreme Wasp #1

Mind Control Jewel wasps have powerful venom. It turns cockroaches into zombies. Female jewel wasps inject venom into a cockroach's brain. This makes the cockroach unafraid of the wasp. The wasp leads the cockroach into her nest. Once they are in the nest, the female wasp lays a single egg on the cockroach's leg. Then she leaves the nest and seals the entrance shut. After the egg hatches, the larva will eat the zombified cockroach!

GLOSSARY

antennae – body parts that protrude from the head and are used for sensing surroundings

nectar – a sugary fluid produced by plants

predators – animals that hunt and eat other animals

species – a group of living beings that are closely related

venom – a poison produced in an animal's body

RESOURCES

Grissell, Eric. *Bees, Wasps, and Ants: The Indispensable Role of Hymenoptera in Gardens*. Portland, Oreg.: Timber Press, 2010.

Schmidt, Justin O. *The Sting of the Wild*. Baltimore, Md.: Johns Hopkins University Press, 2016.

"Stinging Insects 101." Pest World.org. http://www.pestworld.org/news-hub/pest-articles/stinging-insects-101/.

"Wasps." National Geographic Animals. https://www.nationalgeographic.com/animals/invertebrates/group/wasps/.

INDEX

Praying mantises hunt wasps.

They eat only the protein-rich thorax and discard the rest.